REDBIRD

A Memoir

Heidi Peters

CROSSLINK
PUBLISHING

Redbird: A Memoir

D CrossLink Publishing
C www.crosslinkpublishing.com

Copyright, © 2013 Heidi Peters

ISBN 978-1-936746-82-8

Library of Congress Control Number: 2013950501

Scriptural quotations are taken from the NEW AMERICAN STANDARD BIBLE copyright © 1960, 1962, 1963, 1968, 1971, 1972, 1973, 1975, 1977, 1995 by The Lockman Foundation. Used by permission

Praise for REDBIRD: A Memoir

Spiritual, Inspirational, and a Must-Read! Heidi Peters provides the reader with a plethora of emotions while telling her unique and heart-warming story. Revealing her soul for the world to see is bravery at its best! *Vito DiSalvo, Composer, Managing Partner, Mifflin Hills Music Publishing*

Heidi Peters unashamedly opens up the most intimate part of her heart. Upon meeting Heidi, I was caught up in the excitement of a contagious desire to share her love of God and the life lesson of peace and gratitude that she wants to share. A peaceful quick read for a dose of "Sonshine." *Debra Bates, RN, Coordinator of Health Ministries, Christ United Methodist Church, Bethel Park, PA*

This book truly captured the feelings and devastation of early loss and grief when Heidi's beloved uncle died suddenly. She describes how the deep pain and loss turned her to her faith in a loving God. This book is about hope, healing, and love. *Lillian L. Meyers, Ph.D, Psychologist, Grief Educator, Author, and Bereaved Mother*

To John J. Broman

For my Dad

and

Allison and Owen

"He will cover you with His pinions,
and under His wings you may seek refuge."

(Psalm 91:4)

Prologue

Every creature has a purpose, and it took thirty-four years for me to find mine. I was one of those kids who wouldn't hurt a fly. Having all boy cousins, I always came to the quick defense of lightning bugs and worms. I was an only child in a family whose pets over the years consisted of a shaggy white mutt, a hamster, a rabbit, fish, a stray litter of kittens we had rescued, and a bulldog. Thankfully, my parents supported my sensitive, nurturing personality. My Uncle Rick—Ricky to me—lived next door, and he would fire his BB gun at groundhogs. Praise the Lord, he missed; or at least that is what I was told. I often tried to push my dad in a different direction. For instance, one day, when I was twelve years old, a groundhog was an unwelcome guest under our deck. At my urging, my father borrowed a live trap from a friend and took the critter down to the river to set it free, barely escaping an attack by the enraged fellow! Even at that young age, I instinctively sought to rescue animals—whether they appreciated my efforts or not.

Maybe my parents should have named me after Francis, the patron saint of animals, because of my connection and devotion to all creatures. Where did my natural affinity with animals come from? I was about to find out.

I have always been told that my Grandma Susan was a softy in the biggest sense of the word. My grandfather supported her love for animals just as my parents supported mine. Grandma had three sons—Evan, Johnny, and Ricky; a big lovely ranch-style home filled with beautiful things; and seven dogs, a cat, and a lamb. One day, Ricky brought a kitten (later named Kitty) home in a baseball cap, and Grandma readily conceded when he asked, "Mom, can we keep it?" When Grandma left this world, her beloved dog, Tarzan, took off shortly after. He never came back. This wasn't much of a surprise to the family, because Tarzan had always sat at my grandmother's feet. If she moved from the chair she was in, Tarzan tagged right along with her. Somehow, it was fitting that after Grandma's homegoing, he too should move on.

Although I never had the opportunity to meet my Grandmother Susan, I feel as though I know her well. She loved birds, and so do I. Her sterling silver decorated with etchings of birds, Hummel bird figurines, and other bird collectibles have been passed on to me and are all sweet reminders of her. Birds are simple and pure. Each of their markings is a stroke of God's paintbrush, creating perfection. Nothing, however, matches the beauty of the redbird, because it is colored by God's love. This is where my story begins. I thought my journey would take me far away from where I started, but I am finding that my heart's desire is leading me back to my roots. Not surprising, a redbird points the way home.

Christmas Chaos

As I look back on my childhood, Christmas seems very different from my perspective as a thirty-four-year-old than when I was only four. Life seemed so much simpler then. It is probably unfair for me to compare myself to my mother, especially because, these days, not too many full-time stay-at-home moms are left. Working part-time outside our home and being in charge of our tight budget were two challenges I faced as a parent. With so much to juggle, everyone I knew—and even those I didn't know—could tell with one look how I felt about the Christmas season. With my dry, flyaway hair, wiped-out appearance, and stiffly held body, I'm sure those around me didn't know whether to run the other way or feel sorry for me as Christmas drew near.

God bless my neighbor, Deb, for her type-A personality and strong faith in the Lord; she always seems to have it together. *"You look tired today,"* she wrote once in an e-mail. *"I said a prayer for you."*

Great! I thought. *Now I look so bad I need a prayer vigil!*

The next day at the bus stop, Deb and I talked about vitamins and probiotics. I was convinced that by taking more vitamins, walking more, drinking extra water, and eating fresh produce, I would be back on track in no time. Deb was always doing kind things for neighbors. How did she have the time? After running around all day reading my Post-it® notes and checking off item after item, I barely had time for myself. You know your life is moving too fast if you still have the price tags on your wedding china after nearly nine years!

Deb slipped me a bag of her homemade healthy treats and a flyer about a Christian radio station that promised to be "inspiring and uplifting." Well, I would have to listen to this new station in the car without my kids around because "inspiring and uplifting" lyrics did not normally find their way on today's pop music channels. I hurried up the street toward home, determined to get this Christmas chaos under control.

The first challenge that greeted me was the forty gifts stacked around my living room. The problem wasn't the mounds of gifts piled all over the floor; it was that most of the gifts had been purchased a year ago at seventy-five percent off during Christmas sales, and I didn't have any gift receipts. I had to hope that each person would like his or her present. But with so many people to buy for, in my opinion, they were lucky to get a gift from us at all. If they didn't like it, too bad; they would be stuck with it. Not exactly the spirit of Christmas, but that's how I felt.

These forty gifts were mixed up in disorderly heaps. They had been laid on the floor for the past twenty-four hours with no clear indication to whom they should belong. The previous night, my husband, Todd, had glanced over from the kitchen after I had sat for hours just staring at these gifts. "Do you think Bob would like the tea set or a blanket?" I asked him.

"Are you overwhelmed?" he responded.

Overwhelmed! I thought. *This is a joke.*

Between buying and wrapping gifts, baking the premade frozen cookie dough I had managed to pick up at the store, decorating the house inside and out, sending cards, and taking care of all things related to Christmas, how could I not be overwhelmed? I refused to battle the portrait studios for the perfect Christmas picture while hearing screaming children and their broken-down parents in the background. Instead, I decided to go to the local drugstore and simply purchase fifty prints of my children, Allison and Owen, looking like they got along in a picture we'd taken the prior year.

Todd was appalled by my new system of mailing cards. Because I wasn't the most organized person in the world, the recipe box that housed all our wedding guests' addresses was an outdated mess. Therefore, Allison was instructed to take over mailing the cards using my brilliant, inspired plan. When a card came in, she was to use the sender's return address and mail our card back to that person or family. *What was wrong with that?* I thought. Christmas was becoming a race I was determined to win. Secretly, I was hoping to at least cross the finish line.

I could never really complain about the Christmas chore list. By the time I grumbled about all the wrapping to be done, I was cut off. More than wanting someone to take pity on me, I just wanted help—and a lot of it. It seemed as though the only ones who really felt my pain were my two cats that joined me in staring for hours at the forty packages on the floor. None of us had an answer to this gift-giving dilemma.

You see, over a span of forty-eight hours, we celebrate Christmas four times with four sets of people. *Is this really normal?* I wondered. I love my relatives dearly, but sometimes I just wanted a peaceful Christmas day with only my husband and kids. I knew the time would come sooner rather than later when the kids would be out of the house.

These forty gifts also meant that forty gifts would be coming our way. So many less-fortunate people needed the basic necessities of life. We were spoiled to have so much. Why couldn't life be simpler? Why did I have to perform a massive overhaul of my house before the holidays to prepare for the bags and bags of new toys and gifts that would be coming our way? I kept thinking, *This is not what Christmas is about.* If only I had known at that moment that I, a part-time bank teller and stay-at-home mom, would have the power to change our chaotic circumstances, I would have had hope. I didn't know yet that we can redirect our hearts no matter what obstacles life throws our way. I was still to discover how to move beyond the chaos to embrace God's purposes for our lives.

As usual, evening came quickly, and I had the kids gobble up some dinner and put on their nice new outfits for the school's Christmas program. There would be no ruffled holiday dresses for my daughter Allison, now twelve. My six-year-old son Owen, however, had picked out his first sports coat all by himself. The coat was red velour, and he looked like a little gentleman in it.

I had been desperately looking forward to their Christmas program. My kids attend Catholic school, and the program always takes place in front of the altar in our beautifully lit and decorated church. It would be a moment of peace that promised to bring me the true meaning of Christmas. Or so I thought.

Arriving at church in our classic five-minutes-late style, we sent the kids off with their classmates and teachers as we hurriedly took our seats. Their grandparents had arrived before us and had saved seats pretty close to the front and on the end. (Maybe when I become a grandma, I will have time to arrive early and save seats.) I pulled out my camera, and my husband had the video camera, which, by a miracle, was charged. Thanks to the Post-it note I had remembered to write two days ago. We were ready to go. I sighed in relief and settled in to enjoy the program.

Because Owen was in kindergarten, his class was set to go first. In a gentle manner, the teacher lined the students up on the risers. I could see big smiles and waving hands. The youngest students were still excited to be performing—not humiliated like the older ones. The music teacher lifted her arms as a cue for the first song to begin. At the sound of the first angelic note, the gates opened and the paparazzi flooded in. My mouth literally dropped open, and my face turned hot and red. As the little ones began to sing, so-called grown-ups rushed down the center aisle of the church and stood directly in front of all of us who were still seated. All I saw were rear ends and bright flashing lights. There was the occasional woman who would look as if she had a bad back as she made a beeline to the front for her shot. She would walk hunched over, thinking she was doing us a favor. My instincts caused me to jump up and hurry to the back of the church where I felt it would be appropriate to stand. How could adults act like this? The principal stood behind the music teacher like an armed guard, so she wouldn't be trampled. I found myself a little hole where I could see my son's precious round face, golden hair, and crimson velour jacket. I tried with all my heart to block the rest of the world out, but before I knew it, the kindergarten class finished and left the stage.

As I took my seat, my eyes filled with tears, but not because of how proud I was of my son. Yes, I was very proud of him, but these tears were caused by the reality that I couldn't escape the Christmas chaos even in the sanctuary of my own church. If I couldn't avoid it there, where could I find the "peace on earth" that Jesus came to bring? I was in a complete daze for the next few performances, keeping my head down and just wanting to go home.

Finally, it was time for Allison's sixth-grade class. Thankfully, no parents in their right minds would dare to rush to the front for this class. The fear that they would be reamed out by their sons or daughters for embarrassing them was enough to keep parents in their seats. No big smiles or waves came from these sixth graders either. This class was all business. They were there to perform the song, or at least lip-sync, and then leave the risers.

At the end of the program, we were all asked to join in one last sing-a-long. Nothing came out of my mouth. It was too hard to sing joyful carols with such a heavy heart. I told the kids they did a fabulous job, but inside I planned on trying to forget this night altogether. Mentally, I prepared what I would e-mail the principal the following morning about the spectacle that had just taken place. Something had to be done so that it would never happen again.

The response from the principal was what I expected: she gave her full support. With one last performance from the kindergarten class at the end of the week, there was a chance to make things right. The play was a reenactment of the birth of Jesus. Owen was Sheep Number Five and knew his lines backward and forward. If I had to go there an hour early for a front-row seat, I would. And I did. The principal put her "stay-in-your-seats" rule in place, and it worked! I began to feel a glimmer of hope and a slight stirring of the Christmas spirit.

After-school Car Line

My early twenties were selfish years—all about fun and the things I wanted. As I grew older, my thirties were selfless years. Maybe it was not completely on purpose. Once you have children, you just don't have time to think about yourself. Your mind is focused on your family.

I grew up going to church, but by the time I got to college, Sunday mornings were for sleeping in after a weekend of social gatherings. Some of us referred to Sunday evenings as Sunday-night drama, because the girls would fight about what had happened over the weekend. Looking back, I don't know how I could have let things go on that way for four years. I suppose we are all on a journey and that we should be continuously learning and growing with each decision we make. Graduating five months pregnant and single after the break down of a senior year relationship, I gave birth to my daughter and got my life in order.

I eventually married my kindergarten sweetheart who adopted Allison and loved her as his own. We moved to Bethel Park, a suburb of Pittsburgh. I will never forget the comment Allison made to my parents as they were ready to drive off after moving us into our new home: "Pap, who will take care of me?" Up until that point, Allison was used to me trudging off to work while my parents stayed behind to babysit. This was a reminder of the impact my parents had on

Allison in helping me raise her for the past three years. After my teary-eyed dad explained the new arrangement, in a business-like manner, he told his three-year-old granddaughter to call him if she needed anything.

My daughter began to attend the local Catholic school. We became involved in helping at the school and went to church as a family. The parish had decided to move from its old school building into a modern and efficient new building on the same property. The old building was leveled after the completion of the new. I was excited about the future that this school would provide for my daughter. I liked the fact that God was an integral part of my daughter's learning curriculum. It was important to me that the values we taught at home were being reinforced at school.

The school became a second family. When my son was old enough to enter, we considered moving our daughter to public middle-school because of our stretched budget. An anonymous school family offered to pay her tuition to keep her there. This act of pure goodness changed my life. At that moment, I could only write a thank-you note from my heart to this family; the principal cried after she read it. To this day, I continue to think of this blessing and give thanks in my prayers for this family and their generosity. I determined that if I were ever in the position to help someone as these people had helped my family, I would jump at the chance. What I did not fully understand at the time was that I didn't need to be in a better position financially to make a significant difference in someone's life. Little steps taken faithfully can lead to the mountaintop.

So here I was on a cold December day, waiting in the car line circle to pick up my son, knowing I would be back two hours later for my daughter. Busy from morning until night, I loved this blessed time as I waited in the car line. I would sit with my windows up and music blasting, enjoying these few moments to myself.

For the most part, those who attend private schools come from families that can easily afford to pay the tuition. I watched many moms, in their heels and fashionable attire, exit luxury vehicles as they came to pick up their children. Their "perfection" was just one more reminder of my messy existence. *At least I have the bigger car today with the power locks and windows,* I thought. I forgot what I had taught my children: we are created the same because everyone can choose to carry God's goodness within. There on my seat was Deb's flyer about the radio station that played inspiring, uplifting music. I owed it to myself to check it out, and, when I did, I heard a song sung by JJ Heller titled "Your Hands." It brought tears to my eyes.

Normally, I prayed for many things but seldom for myself. My prayers usually included requests for God to keep stray cats and outdoor animals warm in the winter. I would pray for abused people to be numb to the pain inflicted by their abusers. I prayed for God to keep my family safe. And I always prayed for my dad. Ever since I was little, I had feared losing him while I was still young—just as he had lost his parents. But as I heard that song in that moment, I prayed an openhearted, honest prayer. I wanted to feel God's presence so strongly in my life that no matter how shaken I might be by life's tragedies, I would always know I was held in God's hands. As I quickly wiped the tears from my eyes, I spotted my little ball of sunshine. In my sweats and tennis shoes, I jumped out of the car to get the hug I so desperately needed from Owen. And off we went.

A Sunday Drive

O ne day, I asked friends whom we hadn't seen in a while to come over for a get-together. Most normal people would say, "Do you want to stop by this weekend?" I, however, had asked if they wanted to come from 6:00 to 8:00 PM on February 2, which was a day in the middle of the week, some six weeks away. This was how we planned our lives. We had to jump on these little windows of time like an avid shopper deftly snatching the last sale item off the shelf. The days filled up quickly with the kids' activities, holiday parties, appointments, and constant errands, so it wasn't unusual for special days to be planned months in advance.

That was the case on this particular Sunday. My parents, husband, kids, and I were going to drive into Pennsylvania Amish Country to the town of Smicksburg, about a two-hour drive from our home. I looked forward to this day as some would anticipate a week's vacation at the beach. Maybe, for once, I could slow down time and find a way to relax. The night before our big day out, I reminded Todd of our scheduled trip. I was not the least bit surprised by his response: "Where are we going?"

The poor guy always got up at the crack of dawn and would come home after a ten-hour day five days a week to coach the kids' teams and run them around. I'm sure nothing would please him more than to be stuck in a minivan for a total of four hours worth of driving, only to find himself in a barn full of country crafts, furniture, and handmade décor. At least my parents would treat him to a great meal on the way home, a reward that would consist of meat and potatoes—not the burnt, organic vegetarian meals I offered the family at our house.

I'm usually not a morning person, but on that day, I was bright and chipper. The kids had no idea where we were going. They were just happy to see their grandparents. We all piled into the minivan and took off for our country drive. With all the bad weather we had been experiencing, we were especially blessed with a beautiful sunny day. My dad mentioned we were going to go right by Indiana University of Pennsylvania, where he had gone to college along with my Uncle John—Johnny to me. My dad and Johnny were only fifteen months apart, and, for a time, roomed together at school. My Grandmother Susan also attended IUP when it was called Indiana State Teachers College.

My grandmother grew up on a farm before it was developed into the neighborhood in which I grew up. Her parents would tie a red bow in her hair and watch as she ran down to her Aunt Kate and Aunt Suz's house. I took the same steps years later, running through the field to Ricky and Weezy's, my uncle and aunt who eventually took over the house. While I was a single mother living with my parents, my daughter traced the same path. I find it so sweet in life that even though we may not share the same time together on earth, we can share the same experiences.

My grandmother ended up running down there so often that in the end, her two aunts practically raised her. Aunt Kate and Aunt Suz never had a lot of money. They cleaned houses to help put my grandmother through college. It was quite an honor for a young woman to be able to go to college at that time. My family has letters that the aunts had written my grandmother as she completed her teaching degree. Years ago, I found a letter that brought tears to my eyes as I was cleaning out a closet full of pictures. In this letter to her two sons in college, my grandmother talked of Ricky, the youngest, being sick but not wanting her help and still making it to play in his high-school football game.

Ricky was the athlete, and my dad and Johnny were the musicians. They both went to IUP for music, and it was a good thing, because academics were not their strong suit. My dad, the worrier, would call home and say, "Mom, I'm anxious about this class. It's really tough." Johnny, the free spirit, would say, "Mom, everything is great. Classes are easy and I'm meeting a lot of people." Then he would hang up the phone, look at my dad, and say, "I'm failing everything." I'm sure my grandmother knew of their academic struggles. She finished her letter by saying, *"Well, study hard. Success is not an accident. Love, Mum."* This framed letter hangs in my dining room next to my grandmother's tea cart and beautiful china. Finding this letter was like hearing my grandmother's voice, and it taught me how important it is to take the time to write from your heart.

As we pulled onto the college campus that day, I could see in my dad's eyes how much he loved it there. He showed us the music hall and where some of his classes were held. I'll never forget the moment he talked about how he and Johnny lived in Whitmeyer Hall and later in a house on campus. I asked him to get out of the minivan so I could take a picture of him in front of the building. But he didn't want to because he wanted to head out to Smicksburg. He had no idea that weeks later, he would have to hold back his tears while talking about how closely bonded he was to his brother John as they went through IUP together.

When the kids noticed the first Amish buggy, you would have thought they had seen a flying saucer. "Look! Look!" they screamed. "There's another one!" We started spotting buggies closer and closer together. I wondered what the Amish thought of us. They certainly didn't scream and point in our direction. Their lives were simple and pure like I wanted mine to be. They wore simple clothes, had simple transportation, and a simple wave and smile were all we got in return for our gawking. I began to notice that everything I loved was simple and pure. Whether it was birds, the Amish lifestyle, the type of music I enjoyed, or the rolling hills of the country, simplicity was what my heart cried out for.

At the most, Smicksburg had six stores that were spread sporadically over a few acres of rolling land. The biggest store, which we visited first, was filled with beautiful handcrafted furniture.

The pride the Amish take in their work was obvious. I was sure the pace at which they lived their lives was not the same as that which we kept in our family. Their attention to detail was reflected in the way they crafted their furniture. When you go through life like it's a race, you miss a lot of precious details. We decided to slow down and enjoy the merchandise. When we did, each piece seemed more precious than the last.

I found a meaningful portrait of a young woman who looked a lot like me. She was showing a child how to feed the birds in the winter. This act of kindness on a dark winter's day expressed to me what Christmas really meant. I left the picture there that day, only to retrieve it later because it meant so much to me. My parents purchased a rocker as a Christmas gift for our family. I knew it would look beautiful in our family room with our other country furniture. We loaded it up, and, as we started toward home, I announced to everyone, "Do you know what my dream house would be? It would be a simple farmhouse that Todd would design to be built on Johnny's property." Johnny lived on a ninety-acre farm near Bentleyville, Pennsylvania. He put his heart and soul into fixing up the eighteenth-century farmhouse and was always so busy working on something at the farm that he even ate standing up. Silently thinking to myself, I considered that maybe Johnny would need someone to check on him when he was older. However, I could not picture him as being old, because he was so full of life.

Many of our friends had built beautiful homes in nice neighborhoods, but my dream house was different. I just never imagined I would have the courage or means to make it a reality. I had told a friend that I liked an original yellow farmhouse that still lingered among the massive new homes surrounding it in her housing development. This farmhouse was so small and quaint she didn't even remember its being there. Her eyes were on bigger and better things. To me, though, this farmhouse was beautiful because it was so pure and simple. My only question to Todd was if he thought I would be afraid to live in the country. It was a far cry from our corner lot in the suburbs. His answer was yes. The truth was that there were some things he didn't know about me, because I didn't even know them about myself quite yet. Maybe my dad knew, because he said, "Tell John."

I said, "No way. Not now." I wish I had.

Christmas Snow

We usually kicked off the holiday season with a Christmas party at Johnny's farmhouse. I looked at it as another minibreak before the final countdown to Christmas. The night we drove there was the start of a heavy snow, the likes of which Pittsburgh hadn't seen in decades. I was determined to get there, so we followed my parents in their four-wheel-drive vehicle. It's funny how kids think sliding all over the road is an exciting adventure. We made it to Evans Road. I always remembered this little gravel road leading up to the farm, because my dad and grandfather were both named Evan. As we pulled up to Johnny's yellow stucco farmhouse, the snow danced through the air. After we all walked into the house, Johnny said, "If you go any slower, the temperature will drop ten degrees in here." Johnny always hated the winter. I told him that all the snow added to the ambiance, but he didn't look convinced.

The same people always attended Johnny's Christmas parties; some I saw only once a year. We would say our polite hellos and then pretty much stay with the group we had come with. The farmhouse had three fireplaces: one in the master bedroom, one in the original sitting room, and one in a beautiful new addition. Johnny always had a string of colored Christmas lights on the mantle, but that was the extent of his Christmas decorating. He did, however, show off every Christmas card that was sent to him. That was Johnny. He proudly displayed anything anyone ever got him. The tractor couch-throw I had given him a few years ago was draped on the back of a rocker that looked just like the one my parents had bought for us in Smicksburg. He had dozens of pictures of good friends, family, his dogs, Tami (his horse from years ago), race cars, and tractors—all the things that made up the precious details of his life. He framed a note to his parents that he had written when he, his brothers, and a cousin had run away for a night. It said:

Dear Mom and Dad,

I got hungry for adventure. Don't worry, won't go far away. Be back tomorrow. Hope you won't be mad.

John, your son.

P.S. We dressed warm enough.

I think Ricky threatened to tell on them at the last minute if they didn't take him, too. Grandmother Susan saved that note in her safety deposit box, and I'm glad she did.

I reached into my bag and took out some crackers and a cheese ball that my Aunt Maureen, my mom's sister, had made because I never had a chance to make anything. We thought the kids might be able to sled ride, and thinking they could use something hot to drink afterwards, I pulled out some hot chocolate mix and organic soy milk I had brought with me. Being the bachelor he was, I didn't know if Johnny would have any milk. Furthermore, I was concerned about his spring water at the time even though it was probably a million times better than the water I got from my own sink. I threw the soy milk in his fridge, and he looked at me as if I was nuts.

I should have been completely relaxed—the farm usually did that for me—but I was still uptight about Christmas. I suppose Weezy was too, because we decided to forego exchanging gifts between our families next year as it was becoming too excessive. We would rather donate to charity. She told me she couldn't get into the spirit of the holiday season either this year, and she would be glad when it was over. It made me sad to hear that, even though I felt the same way. I wonder now if perhaps, between the two of us, we sensed something bad was soon to happen.

We listened to Christmas music on the way home, and I heard "The Gift" sung by Aselin Debison. The song was about an orphan girl who rescued a wounded bird. The bird was all she had to give to Jesus for Christmas, and she was ashamed. The little bird took flight and sang the most angelic music as a gift for Jesus. The car was dark, and no one knew I cried most of the way home.

Our little window of time for Mass would be on Christmas Eve. Our neighbors offered to save seats for us because everyone who didn't go to church all year showed up for Christmas Mass. I don't know why that bothered me, considering I used to be the same way.

Todd took Owen up to see the manger, and Allison and I sat quietly waiting for Mass to begin. I cried during "Silent Night." I wondered why I was being so emotional about Christmas this year. Everything was spinning, and I felt no one understood me.

We had a quiet Christmas Eve dinner with just the four of us, because we were celebrating Christmas at my sister-in-law's home with Todd's side of the family the day after Christmas. Allison and I would have to meet Owen and Todd there because she was in a basketball tournament that we had already committed to before the date for our family get-together had been changed. It would be another marathon race. I fell asleep as soon as my head hit the pillow that night. Christmas morning took off as soon as our feet hit the floor. We had an itinerary to stick to, and we stayed on target. The kids opened their gifts at our house. We sat under our Christmas tree, which I had decorated with beautiful ceramic birds and berries. Our tree was one part of Christmas that I had managed to keep simple. Two jeweled redbirds were my favorite ornaments on the tree. We got dressed in our holiday attire, packed the car, and were off to my parents' house. Todd's parents would be there too, as well as my dad's side of the family.

After most of the guests left, we moved to the family room to open more gifts. Ricky, Weezy, and Johnny stayed and watched. They stayed much longer this year than usual, and it was really nice. Time went by at its normal pace, and we had some good, crazy laughs. While my mom's side of the family is like a pretty shade of beige, my dad's side is a bit more colorful. We finished the day at my Aunt Maureen's visiting my mom's side of the family. We headed home with a car jam-packed with presents, just as I had anticipated; but at that moment, I knew I had pretty much made it through the holidays.

Bad News

P ure exhaustion was what I was left with when Christmas was finally over. My friend Tina would be in town the week between Christmas and New Year's Day, and I just hoped I would have enough energy to keep my eyes open when she visited.

There was no way I was going out for New Year's Eve this year. Allison would spend her first New Year's Eve without us because she was going to a friend's house. I was extra happy Tina would be stopping by that night because it would help fill the void of Allison's not being home. Allison and her friend reminded me of Tina and me when we first became friends. We were about the same age, and whenever we were together, there were constant giggles and plans for sleepovers.

Todd and I always had two or three offers for New Year's Eve, and usually we would stop by at least a couple of parties. This year, though, I had been able to say no to our friends. So, on New Year's Eve—after Tina left—Todd, Owen, and I sat on the couch in our pajamas and tried to stay up until midnight. I didn't understand why I felt so unsettled and bothered that night. Everyone went to bed, but I was up all night, upset with Todd for no good reason. My nerves were shot, and something was working inside me that I couldn't control.

In a daze, I sat on the couch in the living room, miserable from having had only a few hours of restless sleep. Something caught my eye in the window. I got up to see three redbirds in the bush right up against our house. One was bright red, and the other two were much softer in color. I forgot about my troubles for a second, and then collapsed back on the couch.

It was unusual for Todd and me not to get along, and he left hurriedly in the morning without saying where he was going. I asked Owen if he knew where his dad had gone, but he didn't know either. A few minutes later, the phone rang, and when I answered it, I was greeted with the words, "We have some bad news."

Anytime the conversation started that way, I knew where it was going to end. Those words translated to, "We've had a death in our family." My mom then began to talk about how my Uncle Johnny hadn't been feeling well with his acid reflux lately, and, before she could finish her sentence, I blurted out, "Is he alive?" My mom's voice quivered as she replied, "No."

I screamed and kept screaming unearthly sounds of purely agonizing emotion, the depth of which I had never felt before in my life. I couldn't control what was coming out of me even when Owen ran around the corner. His eyes were filled with fear and tears as he yelled over and over, "What happened?" Just as bluntly as my mom had told me, I told him. He broke down and sobbed.

My mom wanted to come over to be with us. My dad went straight to the farm because Johnny's neighbor, Ralph, had found Johnny collapsed in the bathroom. I told my mom I needed to find Todd and get Allison home, and I didn't want her to come. I called

Allison at her friend's house and told her over the phone that Johnny was dead. I regret the way I told both my children about Johnny's death, but sometimes shock keeps us from thinking rationally. When Todd walked into the house, he entered an atmosphere of pure chaos. Owen and I sat on the couch, crying, as I told Todd the news about Johnny. Even at that moment, I remained in a state of such tremendous shock that I asked Todd to call my mom and ask her if Johnny really was dead. It seemed like a terribly bad dream. Todd tried to give me a hug that I didn't want. I was numb and frozen.

Allison got a ride home and fell into Todd's arms as he met her on the front porch. Owen was inconsolable and cried for two straight hours until he was exhausted. With nothing else to say or do, I somehow made it to my room from which I wouldn't move for two days.

Now I know what "paralyzed with grief" means. I stayed there in bed for forty-eight hours. I barely slept, and I didn't eat, shower, or move. Whenever I was awake, tears streamed down my face to the point that my eyes were just about swollen shut. The kids looked at me from a distance as they walked down the hall and asked if I was okay. I know they were afraid, but I simply couldn't help them. At that moment, I felt as if I was in the darkest place of my life. I could barely think. I just knew that I wanted help. I would never desert my family. I wanted Todd to take me to the hospital, and I wanted someone to fix me. I worried that losing my dad might break my heart enough to kill me. Todd just sat with me and said nothing, comforting me in the best way he could.

Saturday night, when I could take no more, silent screams filled my head. I was calling for my uncle as loudly as someone stranded alone on a mountaintop would scream, desperate to be rescued. A short time later, our cats, Sunny and Cleo, walked through my bedroom door. Sunny crept along as though she were afraid; she slowly looked up at one part of the ceiling and then over to the other side. There was not a sound or anything there for her to see. My world stopped for a moment as I focused on her. Sunny was a rescued cat, and I knew she was devoted to us from the way she looked into our eyes when we called her name. It was as though she could see straight into our souls. Right then, she stared past me toward my closet as if someone were standing there; she had the same intense look that she always gave when she looked into a person's eyes. She stared intently for a few minutes, and then both cats curled up next to me as though whatever Sunny had seen was gone.

I got angry. I was furious. I felt as though I was stupid and naïve, looking for a sign when there was none. Johnny was gone; I had to face the truth. But at that moment, the deep depression and heaviness in my chest abruptly filled with a joy that I had never felt before on earth—not even during my happiest times. Time stood still. As I wavered on what I had or had not seen, my mind fought what my heart was feeling. My mind and body were no longer functioning as one. I was crying with unimaginable sadness, but my heart felt as if it were about to leap out of my chest.

Feeling completely weightless, I questioned whether I should get up and run. I felt ready to compete in a marathon, but I refused to move, afraid this feeling would slip away. My mind started to catch up with my heart, and I finally stopped crying. I stayed there in my bed completely frozen.

I knew that what I felt was real. Johnny wasn't gone; he just could no longer be here with us. I knew this peace was what it was like to be in heaven in God's hands. Although I hadn't seen heaven, I felt it in those moments. I knew that Johnny was experiencing this same energy and was celebrating in God's presence with all the ones we had lost before him.

God knew I was at my darkest moment. I had prayed only one month earlier for Him never to leave me in my worst time of despair. I wanted to know what it felt like to be in His hands.

Jesus said that when we cry out to Him for mercy, He will not turn us away. Before He went back to heaven, Jesus told His friends that He was giving them a gift of peace. *And the peace of God, which surpasses all comprehension, will guard your hearts and your minds in Christ Jesus.* (Phil 4:7) He gave me a true peace, and I believe my uncle was there with me at that precise moment. God used my love for Johnny and my love for animals to heal me from the inside out with His mercy.

I held onto this feeling until I fell asleep. I knew these emotions couldn't last forever, but I would always carry with me the reality of what happened. I would never let this gift be wasted. I would cherish and hold onto it forever; I refused to let my life slip by me so quickly without fulfilling my purpose or making a difference in other people's lives. I was far from perfect, but God loved and accepted me. I would not judge others, and I would help someone else as He had helped me.

Johnny had rescued any animal that walked down his long driveway, and I felt that same compassion for animals. Sunny's full name was Sunshine Windhaven. I never would have imagined that her name would take on so much more significance after Johnny's death. In the biggest of storms, God is still unshakeable. He is a safe haven. Animals are God's creation, and Sunny was put in my path for a reason. Unknown to me at the time, my Uncle Johnny and this little rescued barn cat would be two inspirations in my new plan to make a difference in the world—no matter how big or small. They would always be a part of my purpose. More than anything, I just wanted everyone to know that Johnny was okay, and now so was I.

A New Day

I felt like a child again. I had no fears, no worries, and no exhaustion. A weight had been lifted, providing me with a new energy that I had never before experienced as an adult. Just as Jesus told Nicodemus, "Truly, truly, I say to you, unless one is born again he cannot see the Kingdom of God" (John 3:3), I felt as if I had been born again. Even in the midst of my grief, I was experiencing a new kind of life and was stronger than ever before.

I had talked to my dad only once since my uncle had passed. Dad asked if I was okay, and I told him how sorry I was that this had happened to him. I never want to lose my dad, but I also didn't want to see him go through the pain of losing one of his brothers. Growing up, they were as close as brothers could be, and, when they were still in their twenties, they had faced the loss of their parents. They were bonded for life not only through tragic times but endless good times as well.

For me, losing my uncle was like losing a part of my dad. I remember talking to my dad the morning Johnny was found by his neighbor, Ralph. Before Dad got Ralph's phone call, he had told me, "I'm real worried about John." When Dad got to the farmhouse, it was too late. Sitting on the bathroom floor, he held his brother and talked to him. I wish with all my heart that my dad hadn't had to go through that painful experience, but that is the kind of man my father is—selfless.

I have always gone to my dad for anything, but knowing what he must have been going through, this was the first time I couldn't go to him with my problems. He had no idea how troubled I was. With my heart finally healed, I couldn't wait another moment to call my dad. I would often talk to him about his parents and how we would be reunited one day. He would always say, "That would be nice." I believe he trusted in God, but, like all of us humans, he had his moments of doubt.

I told him every detail of what had happened to me. At first, he was silent but then he said, "I believe you." I knew with all my heart that what he said was true. Giving him the comfort of knowing that my uncle was safe in God's hands was more important to me than my own peace. Now, we would have the strength to carry on with Johnny's funeral and celebrate his life. There would be many tears in the next few days, but only because we missed Johnny.

It turned out that the people I saw at Johnny's Christmas parties were the same ones I would cling to as they shared story after story about Johnny over the next few days. Johnny had a sort of second family in the town of Bentleyville. He would host a breakfast every Sunday morning that his Bentleyville friends would attend. Mostly men would come. They would attempt to solve the world's problems, eat and drink what they shouldn't, and escape temporarily from the responsibilities of their lives. A man with long hair, jeans, and a T-shirt came to the funeral home when we were about to leave on the first night. I heard him tell his young daughter that Johnny would feed everyone breakfast. I guess he must have, because it seemed as if the entire town of Bentleyville came to the viewing.

In the past, I had judged the women from our private school for their luxury cars and designer clothes, but I learned never to judge Johnny's friends who looked so different from us in their jeans and flannel shirts—some even with ponytails. Grown men, breaking down with tears in their eyes, clearly showed how much they loved Johnny. I wasn't able to look in my uncle's casket because I wanted my last memory of him to be that of taking Owen for a ride on his tractor.

My mom and I smiled at each other when some of Johnny's Bentleyville friends said, "That doesn't look like John." My uncle was buried in the suede sports coat that he wore to every wedding and funeral. In fact, we found the bubble solution from my wedding in his pocket. His friends, however, had never seen him in anything but jeans and a T-shirt. He always wore a pair of red suspenders and a straw hat. His red suspenders were buried with him. I had a beautiful arrangement of sunflowers, wheat, and wildflowers brought in that reminded me of the farm. One florist told me I would never find sunflowers in January, but I didn't give up until I found them. His viewing was in a beautiful old funeral home in downtown Bentleyville. The room we were in had a large mural of a farm. I remember my mom saying, "There's your farmhouse," as she caught me staring at this picture that I wished I could step into for a moment. Johnny knew the funeral director well because Johnny had always played taps at the veterans' funerals. Later, at an emotional ceremony, the veterans would present Johnny with a medal, and the family with a Bible. His trumpets were beautifully displayed, and a collage of pictures sat on an easel. I remember looking at the photos and saying that I had some catching up to do. So many pictures we took in my family were posed or planned, but the pictures of my uncle captured his life in motion. There was a beautiful picture of his farm, and, as I looked closely, there stood Johnny, my dad, and me when I was a little girl. It took a long time before I could look at that picture and not cry.

We had dinner at the club where he had spent so much of his time. His friends put together a huge spread of food for us. I remember driving home that night through terrible weather. As we pulled into our driveway, I saw Sunny's little orange face in the window, waiting for us and making sure we had made it safely home.

The day of my uncle's funeral, I decided I wanted to wear red. It was very important to me that my children wore red also. I had been in such a dark place after learning about Johnny's death. And now, while feeling such overwhelming support and love from God, I couldn't wear black. After the night God came to me, I wanted to let everyone who loved my uncle know how fulfilled he was now. I wrote a letter to my uncle describing that night, hoping I could talk about that moment at the funeral. I had told the reverend about my amazing experience. He counseled me that faith should be shared, but I didn't know if I had the strength to tell everyone about it.

A good friend of my uncle's from college asked the family if he could eulogize John. We were blessed to have him speak. He told of many great times the two of them had shared in college. He referred to my uncle as "wild man John," his little fraternity brother. I could see him slip away into his memories as he described the two of them going to music gigs together some forty years ago. He talked about how great of a heart my uncle had. He said he was the craziest, sweetest man he had ever known.

I smiled, knowing Johnny's goodness couldn't hide under his crazy ways. I was well aware of my uncle's wild adventures with his friends; however, my memories of him were sweet and innocent. Some of my fondest memories with Johnny at the farm included riding in a dune buggy while picking wild flowers out the window, flying kites, spending time with all his animals, having reunions, enjoying bonfires, and watching Owen burst with pride as he rode the tractor while sitting on Johnny's lap. All these great times spent with family and friends were so important to Johnny, and to us. I can't forget Allison's comment: "Pap, I have a great idea! You buy a horse, Johnny can take care of it, and I can ride it!"

I didn't have the courage to stand up in front of such a large crowd of Johnny's friends and family that day, but I watched my dad do it. He never left Johnny's side during the funeral, and he looked stronger to me than I had seen him in years. He greeted every friend and family member who came to see his brother John.

Bob, one of my dad's good friends, arranged to have five trombonists play at Johnny's service. It was unbelievably moving, and it felt as if my dad was playing to him. My dad spoke of how overwhelmed he was to have such support from Johnny's friends and extended family. He recalled a time when he and my mom picked Johnny up at the airport: Johnny came off the airplane wearing a funny hat and crazy outfit. He had his arm around a priest. My mom told him she would wait for my dad and him in the car. At the time, my mom may have had trouble with Johnny's spontaneity, but this recollection brought smiles to our faces.

I knew if I ever again had the chance to speak about someone I loved, I would not hold back; I didn't like the feeling I was left with after saying nothing. I reminded myself, however, that I had been able to talk to several people I was close to over those days, sharing with them my thoughts about my uncle and my faith in my own way.

I buried my letter with Johnny. I knew God had brought us together one last time so that there would be no regrets. Still, I wished I would have spent more time with him at the farm in spite of my busy life.

I stood in the cemetery on January 6, 2010, the day of Epiphany. I felt that in the weeks leading up to my uncle's death, God remembered my cries to Him. The night I cried out to my uncle, God shined His light on me. As the snow filled the bitter cold air, we placed red roses on his casket. I remember my dad telling me how Johnny hated this type of weather, but the snow was pure and meaningful to me. Isaiah 1:18 says:

"Come now, let us reason together", says the LORD. "Though your sins are as scarlet, they shall be as white as snow; though they are red like crimson, they will be like wool."

We have all made mistakes in our lives, but if we allow our hearts to be wide open to Christ, He will cleanse and redeem us.

As we were making our way into the restaurant for the wake, I passed my Uncle Ricky and his son Trevor. I gave them both a strong hug. I couldn't remember the last time I'd hugged them, and I hated to see their hearts breaking. I was thankful that I could remember the last hug I gave Johnny. He never missed one of my parties. I could always count on him to be there. Family was extremely important to him. He parked his Corvette® on the corner of my busy road, and I thought he was crazy. There were certain things he just didn't care about. He got out of the car with a big pecan pie, one of my dad's favorites, and I gave him a big hug. I'm so glad I did.

The day ended, but in a strange way I didn't want it to. I had never been through a funeral with so much support, and I knew that things would now be quiet. As my life moved on, I realized how important it would be to never forget the days after I lost Johnny. Deuteronomy 4:9 reminds us:

> "Only give heed to yourself and keep your soul diligently, so that you do not forget the things which your eyes have seen and they do not depart from your heart all the days of your life; but make them known to your sons and your grandsons."

Things, however, wouldn't be as quiet as I thought they would be, because my heart would start to speak to me.

Breakfast Club

Many years ago, my good friend, Deb, gave me a devotional written especially for mothers. I don't think I was ready for the book at the time, so it was shoved onto one of my bookshelves with the many other books I never had a chance to read. But something had changed in my life now, and I frantically sorted through book after book, searching for it. Finally, there it was! As I grasped the book, the pages fell open naturally to a beautiful prayer in the middle section of the devotional. I could barely trust what my eyes were seeing. This particular prayer discussed how God was able to touch what no other person or thing could touch. I knew from experience that God could heal us from the inside out. I started to understand how God places moments in our lives to show us His constant presence. Just like a patchwork quilt, one beautiful pattern is linked to another to create a blanket of warmth.

I reconsidered going with Deb to a women's Bible study at her church. In the past, I had never seemed to have time for another commitment, but I attended my first Bible study of the new year with Deb and was welcomed with a huge breakfast and many friendly faces. I'm sure the women had no idea what brought me to their church, but each new lesson seemed to run parallel with my life. If your heart is open to Christ, it is amazing how the Scripture can come to life. Even though I was unable to navigate through my Bible in a systematic way,

Bible study was a way to have a true understanding of what the Scripture meant as it was applied to my everyday moments. Every Tuesday morning, my new friends and I got together for our version of a breakfast club where we would put our lives on hold as we looked at the world's problems, shared stories and faith, and gathered for breakfast.

Johnny had had his own version of the breakfast club at his farm every Sunday morning. I had two crocks he had given me that read: "Breakfast Club, BC established 1990." The second one I received from him was the last Christmas gift he would ever give me. I gave him some treats for his breakfast club and a Christmas serving dish with a redbird on it, which I would later see on display at the farm. I can still remember him handing me the crock and telling me how to make pickles. I wasn't so sure that I was a pickle maker at the time, and, as my eyes started to drift, he told me I could put anything into it that I wanted. When I visited the farm after he passed, I stopped at a small Amish shop, and, without realizing the connection, bought a jar of pickles. I am now determined that before I leave this earth, I will be a recreational pickle maker. Johnny always had a pantry full of homemade canned goods for the guys at the breakfast club. Anytime we would go up to visit, he would send us home with something. He kept a sign-in log at his breakfast club that each member would sign at the beginning of their meeting. Our Bible study sign-in log was a prayer list where each woman shared a situation that we could all keep in our prayers and hearts.

In his log, Johnny would always write words from "the Master," his nickname. These few sentences would be comments about life around him, little life-learning lessons, and sometimes just good humor. While some of these messages could move you to tears, some were so wild I wouldn't share them with my closest friend. That was my uncle—the craziest, sweetest man on earth.

From 10-27-02: "45 degrees. Fear is an emotion that will bring you to your knees. You must fight it as you would fight the devil."

And on 1-29-06: "42 degrees. The hardest thing about doing nothing is knowing when you're through."

As I read his words, in a strange but very clear way, I could apply them to my breakfast club. At one of our meetings, we discussed how important it is to become a Good Samaritan. I knew that given my recent experience, volunteering would become a very important part of my life. We discussed the question of: with so many of us needing help in today's world, how should you choose a mission that is right for you? Oftentimes, what brings you to tears will lead you in the direction you need to follow. Helping someone can be uncomfortable, even scary, but a Good Samaritan doesn't turn his or her head to escape the pain of that moment.

My love for animals, just like my uncle's, would lead me to volunteer for the local animal shelter in our area. Every Tuesday afternoon, Allison, Owen, and I would drive out to the pet store and spend an hour or so with the cats waiting to be adopted. We would play with them or simply hold them, giving the love and attention they so desperately needed. I assured my husband that I would not bring them all home, and he often went with us. Even though I felt that this act was just a simple, small way of helping, it did make a difference to the lives of the animals and the lives of my family. Allison and Owen worked together as a team. I loved what I was seeing, and it made my heart very happy. I'd never read the words in Johnny's log book before he passed, but they were meant for my eyes to see. His messages were a reminder that so many people are intertwined in your life as part of God's plan.

His words were also a connection to my grandparents. He wrote in the log on Father's Day, 2003: "Thanks, Dad, for the talent, the work ethic, the honesty, the high standards, and the go for your dreams, the farm, IUP, and the breakfast club. But don't forget that behind every good man is a great woman." April 6, 2003, he wrote: "Mom has been gone for thirty-six years today, and it seems like yesterday. I can still hear her voice. Your second son, John."

I sat on my porch one morning before Deb picked me up for our breakfast club. I've always enjoyed watching the many different birds gather at the bottom of our maple tree to eat their breakfast. The small finches, big blackbirds, redbirds, robins, doves, and the occasional squirrel would all peacefully eat the seeds that dropped from the hanging bird feeder. It always amazed me that there was room for everyone and that they would all share in the feast. This particular morning, I saw a male and female redbird feeding one another. Many times, I have seen a mother or father bird feeding its baby, but this was quite a sight. It was a full proof of God's creation and the goodness He created within them. That very morning at the Bible study, we talked about how the simplest gift of preparing a meal for someone can mean so much, and how important it is to invite everyone to the table. Instead of the little redbird taking the seed for himself, he made sure his partner was full. Over the years, I learned this important lesson in my life and in my marriage.

Whether it was my breakfast club or Johnny's, everyone was welcome—no matter how different he or she might be. I always loved hearing about Blue, Ronnie the Barber, Willie Roach, and Ralph, who were just a few of the unique individuals making up the Bentleyville Breakfast Club. In Luke 14:13–14, Jesus says:

> "But when you give a reception, invite the poor, the crippled, the lame, the blind, and you will be blessed, since they do not have the means to repay you; for you will be repaid at the resurrection of the righteous."

As we broke bread with one another every Tuesday or Sunday morning at our individual breakfast clubs, I know God blessed us both.

Mornings at Johnny's

I remember how overcome with emotion I was when we sold my mother's parents' house not so long ago. Because Grandma Annie could no longer live independently in her home, she had moved into a nursing home. I walked into my grandparents' basement, and every direction I looked conjured another memory. All these memories had been labeled with price tags, which were mostly under five dollars. It pained me to see that at the end of our lives, the things that have meant so much to us can suddenly become a burden for someone else to dispose of.

I felt as though I was losing my breath, so I made a quick exit. As I stood in the backyard crying, my dad came out to comfort me, which was not a surprise. Gently, he tried to lay down the realities of life—never judging me and never losing patience.

From what I've heard, my dad is very much like his dad. From Grandpap Evan, my dad inherited his selfless nature. Grandpap was what you would call "the real deal." Although I've heard many stories about my grandfather, there is one piece of advice that I hold dear to my heart; it gives me incredible strength from Grandpap Evan. He told my dad once that throughout your life, people may use words with which you may not necessarily agree. Your job is to nod your head, smile, and carry on. I've learned how important it is to live your truth and not let the words of others leave you frustrated. Know what words to give power to. Sometimes those words will be yours when God calls on you to speak. A visit from a redbird while thinking of his advice was all I needed to be reminded that Grandpap Evan would always be close by. I thank God for this experience. Dad would say after he lost his father, "If only I could talk to my dad for one minute so I could ask him what to do." I told my dad that by now he knew his father so well he probably already knew what his dad would say. I will likely realize this same thing myself at some point.

One day, I will probably have to go through this sorting process in the house where I grew up, which is unimaginable to me right now—especially if I have to do it without my parents. My mom told me to think about how hard it would be if my grandmother were gone, and we had to go through her things then. I knew she was right. As hard as this task was now, it would have been so much harder under different circumstances.

At Johnny's funeral, I remember telling someone I wanted to go back to the farm alone the first time. I anticipated how difficult it would be. Fully aware of how much I had changed in a matter of days, I knew that the old me would probably never have wanted to go back. The new strength God brought me left me with a yearning to return to the farm where I could be comforted by Johnny's things, knowing he was with God now.

My dad and I went back to the farm together on a bright beautiful morning in the middle of January. As we drove down the long driveway, it felt as if it were my first time there. Because things were different now, I studied every detail that I didn't recall noticing before. I was not thinking of the long list of duties I had to perform that day; I was thinking of how much this farm meant to my family, especially to Johnny. He had an old milk bucket from the previous owners and some other items—timeless artifacts that told a story I would love to know more about. Another treasure was a Bible from the 1800s that I believe was given to my Grandmother Susan from her Aunt Kate and Aunt Suz. Five redbirds appeared in the bush next to my living room window the day I eventually brought that Bible home to display it. Perhaps they were the sweet souls of my grandparents, Aunt Kate, Aunt Suz, and Johnny.

The tears gently flowed for hours as I inspected every last detail of my uncle's house as though I would never be back. My dad assured me there would be plenty of time left for us to come to the farm before any decisions would be made about its future. We sat on the back porch and had a drink together, still stunned by what had occurred. My dad began to realize how much the property meant to me. He told me he would make every attempt to keep a portion of the grounds so that it could be turned over to me.

Once, my dad had asked my uncle why he didn't sell the farm and move to a smaller property. Dad had told him that he could get a great deal of money for it and have much less upkeep. Johnny's simple response was, "I like it here." That was exactly how I felt. Some may have thought that I needed a therapist for thinking that his farm was priceless, but I was beginning to see the similarities that my uncle and I shared. As he had written in his log on 1/13/08: "To be content and to be happy is something that cannot be bought. It goes far beyond wealth."

Throughout our talking and tears, we also enjoyed simple moments of silence. The week quickly passed into the next, and, on another bright sunny morning, we took our routine drive out to the farm. The more I went, the less it hurt to be there. I would see the same little old lady smiling at the restaurant where we would get our breakfast and coffee. I always looked for Hemme, Johnny's cat, while we were there. Ralph assured everyone he would take care of her and made sure that the message made it back to me. He knew Johnny and I were the same with our love and regard for animals. Ralph was one of the very few people to whom I had given a copy of the letter I had written to Johnny. Sadly, Grandma Susan had lost a full-term baby, so there should have been four brothers. In many ways, Ralph was like that third brother to Johnny.

Going to the farm felt like going to the ocean. The untouched land reminded me of a little piece of heaven here on earth. My soul needed to go there. With Johnny leaving this earth so suddenly, I needed time at the farm to adjust to all that had occurred. I looked forward to those mornings all week, and the visits went by so quickly.

My dad drove me around the quaint country town of Bentleyville. I know that parts of this town were not there to impress, but I took the good with the bad and could feel in an instant why Johnny had loved it there so much. My view from those country roads included seeing a picture-perfect creek glistening right alongside the train tracks. The local golf course stood on the hill near the new area high school that had a football field nestled between country farms and rolling hills.

Weeks turned into months, and the time came for me to find the way to Johnny's on my own. My parents informed us that they were going to Florida for a much-needed vacation. I always sat in the passenger seat on our trips to the farm whenever my dad or Todd drove. Riding in the car provided time for me to daydream while my kids were safely belted in with their hands to themselves. I had a few weeks left to practice driving to the farm with my dad. Practice makes perfect, but it was definitely a bumpy ride the first few times. With the sun in my eyes, I almost missed a stop sign, which I would have sailed through if it hadn't been for the loud yell from my dad. Our coffee went flying as I was about to head up the wrong side of the road. At the end of the day, we always had some good laughs. Making mistakes in life reminds us not to make the same mistakes twice, and eventually, I found my way without incident.

With my parents in Florida, the day came when the kids started joining me for my weekly visits to the farm. John Mellencamp was always the soundtrack for our trips, and Owen would play air guitar while we listened to "Jack and Diane."

49

On one of our first trips to the farm, we stopped at the area truck stop to pick up a few snacks. It was apparent we were folks from out of town. Owen could simply not understand it when someone over the loud speaker announced, "Come and get a nice hot shower."

"Did she say shower?" he asked as he giggled. "Why do they want people to get a hot shower?"

The trucker behind us responded, "We're stinky from driving in our trucks all day!"

Allison would always say that she loved the smell of Johnny's house, and I knew what she meant. Maybe it was the fresh air mixed with old history. As we stood on the porch after the grass was freshly cut, we could always smell wild onions.

We hiked to the top of the property to take in the spectacular view. Owen, only six, remembered my parents having picnics up on the hill with him as they waved down to Johnny, who would be on his porch looking up at them through a pair of binoculars. I'm glad he will have those memories.

We walked down to the spring house where Johnny got his water. An antique truck sat in his driveway; it looked like it belonged to The Waltons®. I showed the kids where we hoped to retain fifteen acres in my anticipation to live there someday. They tried to skim for minnows in the small creek that runs through the property. We spotted turkeys, groundhogs, deer, and hawks so big I wondered if they were capable of picking up Owen. And, each time we visited, we would see a redbird. Lately, it seemed as though every wholehearted thought of my uncle would end with my seeing a redbird.

We always finished the day with a pizza from our favorite little country store. Operating his business out of such a small town, the owner knew what had happened to my uncle, and, with our weekly visits, he knew me by name.

There was, however, one trip to the farm that was not as peaceful as the others. I opened the door to see a small black clump on the floor next to Johnny's fireplace. I quickly turned away, fearing what I thought might be a bird. Allison, the bravest, confirmed my fears. I turned to my kids and informed them that it was going to take a team effort in the removal of this bird. Owen, Mr. Sensitive, who is like my little clone, yelled out that he would not be joining our mission. I begged and pleaded with Allison, all the while thinking that maybe I could take off my glasses and blindly remove the bird. Everyone has a phobia; mine would be dead animals, and my children knew that. My daughter sensed my desperation, and, after a bribe of money, she was in. We negotiated down to twenty-five dollars from the original fifty. I reminded her of the time I had cleaned up after her friend had a migraine-induced vomit explosion in our bathroom. I believed I deserved at least half off her original price.

It was time to face our fears, so Allison headed in with a broom and a dustpan. I stood on the opposite side of the room, refusing to look in Allison's direction as I heard her screams: "I can't get it. I

51

can't get it." All I could think of was to yell, "Twenty-five bucks, twenty-five bucks!" Finally, after what seem like an eternity, she got the poor, lifeless bird and ran out of the house. I told her to go to the back of the property, close to all the brush, in order to give the bird a proper and final resting spot. With a shovel in hand, Allison, her skinny little legs flying, took off through the field, yelling, "It's taking too long. It's taking too long." Terrified, Owen ran, staying just inches behind her.

Allison has always been the tough one. She never cried when she got a shot at the doctor, and she was tough on the basketball court and softball field. When she came back down to the farmhouse, I told her to use the bathroom and wash her hands. She anxiously asked if she could wash them at the kitchen sink. Without thinking, I told her it was okay to use the bathroom. I had forgotten she knew that Johnny had been found collapsed in the bathroom, but I was painfully reminded of that fact when she came out of the bathroom and burst into tears. I held her and realized she was my twelve-year-old little girl and didn't always have to be the strong one. If there was ever a next time, I could be brave enough to get the bird. She went out on the back porch to settle down, and I saw Owen rubbing her back. At least I now knew that my children were close in crisis even if they had their routine, normal brother-sister fights.

One morning, my dad, Ricky, and I were out at the farm together. Just like thirty years prior, we were back to dealing with groundhogs. As a family of groundhogs gathered by the creek, Ricky said to my dad, "Should I shoot one?" My dad must have given him a look because he then said, "Should I shoot at it? You know I'll miss." I yelled from the other room, "I'll throw my body in front of it!" Some things never change.

A weekend came when we were miraculously free of kids' activities. As soon as I discovered that open time, I asked Todd to accompany us to the farm for an afternoon. We walked through the woods, and Allison and Todd disappeared deeper into the trees. We were told by family that an abandoned farmhouse and five graves could be found in the dense part of the forest. Years ago, infants died of common illnesses that would be easily treated today, so perhaps that was one explanation for the graves. Once, my Aunt Weezy had walked us through the farm where an old pigpen stood; she told us that the original owners were buried somewhere at the back of the property. She had learned of this when Ricky had taken her on a quad to show her around. Allison was intrigued, but all they came across was a hunting post.

Johnny always hated hunting; however, he eventually let a few friends hunt on the property. I always hated that fact. When we walked through the property with Todd, I knew that what the kids thought were secret hiding spots were actually shelters for the hunters. I refused to go into them and wanted the farm to remain the perfect little world I thought it to be.

When I was up in the attic showing Allison how the farmhouse was completely made of stone under its stucco, we could hear talking downstairs. We came down the steps to find the most countrified man I have ever met in my life. I needed no introduction and walked up to this fireplug of a man in overalls and said, "You must be Blue."

"Yes, I am, honey," he said. I knew Blue came up to collect Johnny's garbage after he died and to check on the place. I also knew he was the primary hunter on the property, and I wished he weren't. Only an hour after seeing the hunter's shelter, I had met the man who used it. I hated what he did, but I immediately loved his endearing kindhearted spirit. Blue was a sweet man with a round face, a sparkle in his eye, and a huge grin. It was almost as if he spoke a different language. He told of how he had grown up on the coal patch. All I had ever heard of was a berry patch, so, as far as I knew, Blue could have lived in the middle of a garden. Later, after asking my husband, I learned that a coal patch was a plot of row houses that coal miners lived in with their families.

Blue picked wild mushrooms, and, unfortunately, marinated them in bacon; otherwise, I would have tried them. He told us he loved growing up in the country and reminisced about how a bunch of his childhood buddies went tic-tacking after taking some corn from the neighbor. I didn't know what that was either but hoped it wasn't illegal.

Blue asked Todd if he had gotten any deer lately, and Todd looked directly at me, saying he didn't hunt. I told Blue I didn't even eat meat, and he said, "That's okay, honey. You don't have to." He probably figured I ate chicken or fish, but he'd have been wrong. I talked to Blue about how I was always told by my dad that Johnny didn't like hunting. Blue confirmed that and told me that when he had asked permission to hunt on the property, Johnny said that he didn't want any wounded animals left out in the woods. Blue stated that Johnny wanted the perfect world, and I took a deep breath because that was exactly how I had felt my entire life. I knew how that feeling could weigh a person down. I thought about Johnny's log entry from 12-03-00:

"To enjoy life to the fullest, you must be content and at peace with the world around you. This is not easy in today's world. You have the final say. I will or will not let this situation get me down, but again it's hard not to keep score. JJB."

I don't suppose Johnny wrote his words with me in mind, but once again, they were meant for me to read.

In a drawer, we found a newspaper article that Johnny had saved. This article became quite fitting for us to see. Johnny must have thought about what was to come when his time on this earth was over. The article was about a farmer without children whose wife had left him. He died alone in his beloved farmhouse, and was found face down on the floor. After his passing, all that was left were the treasured items of his life, which may not have held much value to a stranger at his estate sale. The truth to take away from this story was that the man lived the life he wanted. The small things turned out to be the big things—the important things that make up who you are. I loved the remaining artifacts that represented my uncle's life. I loved them as much as he did.

I know my uncle would not have wanted to leave this earth any other way. The mornings at Johnny's not only helped me learn more about my uncle but also helped me learn more about myself and how much the two of us were alike.

Ruby Tuesday

I'm sure Mick Jagger didn't have a tortoiseshell barn cat in mind when he wrote the lyrics to "Ruby Tuesday." Supposedly, the song was about a groupie who lived a life of freedom—a freedom that was worth the risks that may have come along with this way of existence. To live in a world of rules and structure would have been like living in a cage crushing her spirit. In the end, Jagger's inspiration encouraged him to follow his dreams before he ran out of time. I heard this song the first Tuesday I tried to rescue Hemme, the barn cat, at a time when ruby red was becoming my new favorite color. I began asking myself, "What kind of life would Hemme want?" and, more importantly, "Would she get the chance to decide?"

I don't know why I had been obsessing over what was to become of Johnny's cat, Hemme, since my uncle had passed away. I guess I did know why: I have a soft heart. It was more than just my love for animals; I wanted to take care of the farm, the cat, and anything else Johnny had left behind. His treasures were my treasures, tangible reminders of what I had left of him. Ever since I had received the peace I was looking for after his death, I was a changed person. My husband and my dad told me I was different. But I remember crying to my dad and apologizing for my relapse when I started to be consumed by thoughts of Johnny's cat. I weighed all the options. She would need to be dewormed and vaccinated. If I took Hemme in, I would have to keep the kids out of her way for a while. And what about Sunny? I imagined that Cleo, who didn't have a care in the world, would enjoy a new playmate; however, Sunny would most likely have a complete nervous breakdown if Hemme encroached on her territory. I wondered what Johnny would have wanted.

I had never known where Hemme had come from or even what her name was until Ralph told us. Initially, I thought she was named after the great Ernest Hemingway. I was wrong. One would have to know my uncle to appreciate his humor. Hemme most likely just showed up, as many of his animals did, leading Johnny to affectionately call her his "little pain in the butt"; thus, her full name: Hemorrhoid! My mother, coming from the less colorful side of the family, still prefers to think that Hemme's name derives from more distinguished roots. With my open, caring heart, I could certainly work this situation out. My husband, ever the nice guy, agreed to let me try to bring Hemme in. However, he made me promise to take Ralph up on his offer and give the cat to him if she would rather be outside.

I have always hated making decisions. That was my problem; I wanted a sign and prayed for one. But if God gave us clear directions on how to handle every one of our problems, how would we ever grow and better ourselves? We can't solve and direct the outcomes of our own children's problems, so why do we expect the same from Him?

After multiple phone calls to numerous animal shelters, the vet, and any other cat person I knew, I made the decision to try to bring

Hemme home with us. My dad kept his mouth shut—probably unsure whether my efforts would have a good outcome—but he informed me that he would accompany me on my so-called rescue mission.

Bright and early on a Tuesday morning, I decided to skip my breakfast club and take a ride out to the farm, cat carrier in tow. I was full of good intentions. As my dad and I walked out my front door, three redbirds lined up on the tree branch closest to my front porch; one at a time, each looked directly at us. This was it. This was my sign. I was destined to bring Hemme home and be the owner of three cats. I didn't think that qualified me as a cat lady just yet. For some unsettling reason, I had a knot in my stomach as we drove out to the farm. I was thinking that things are never that easy. I knew that triumphs seldom came without setbacks.

Because I was a bundle of nerves, it was a rough ride out to the farm that morning. It didn't get any better when I let out a big scream after I walked around the house to Johnny's back porch and a massive turkey took off in flight. My dad didn't even have time to relax after our ride before he came rushing to the back porch to see what all the racket was about. We headed inside to the large breakfast table to have our coffee. The beautiful old farmhouse table seated twelve people, but it was just my dad and me that day.

As I was straightening things up in the kitchen, I saw her. Hemme was staring in through the back door while sitting curled up in the sun. Her face was as round as the moon, and when the sun hit her just right, she turned a lovely shade of lilac. I remember telling Johnny how beautiful she was. I knew Johnny had gotten up at 6:00 AM every morning, so they probably met on the back porch while they each enjoyed their breakfast.

Slowly, I opened the door to fill her bowl and then hastily took a seat. Hemme was timid and loved the attention from me as long as I was sitting. My dad watched through the door as I continuously stroked her. He laughed at her tail, which was sticking straight up in the air. All too soon, my impatience kicked in and I just wanted to get the whole thing over with. I wanted to rescue Hemme, keep her warm and fed, and protect her from all the outside dangers. If I had to let the farm go, I would at least have her to hold onto until we built our own farmhouse on those priceless fifteen acres we were going to try to keep. I couldn't wait another second, so I grabbed her with two hands in a lousy attempt to swing her into the cat carrier. She somehow managed to put the brakes on midair and pushed off the palm of my hand with her back paw. Fur went flying as she scurried off and hid under the porch. *She will never trust me again,* was my immediate thought. In addition to worrying about the cat hating me, I began to feel my face becoming red and hot. I felt a burning sensation in the palm of my hand and prayed to God that Hemme hadn't accidentally broken my skin. I nervously examined my hand and found two tiny dots in the middle of my palm. That was all it took to release my old obsessive-compulsive personality.

My dad slid the back door open and said, "We'll try again next time." I was looking directly at him as he calmly advised, "You rushed it. She'll be back." I couldn't concentrate on a word he was saying because my mind was racing with thoughts of how I could lose my hand to infection or contract some horrible disease. He saw my panicked face and asked if she had scratched me. He looked at my hand and tried to quash my fears; he seemed somewhat annoyed at my freaking out about nothing. "Go wash your hands," he directed. Then, he fumbled through the kitchen drawers, found some antibacterial cream that was probably a decade old, and squirted it on my hand.

Once, my dad had watched as Johnny pulled a tick off his head and went on with his day. The old me would have succumbed to fear of Lyme disease, and, unfortunately, the old me was coming back with a vengeance over these two tiny dots on my hand.

Johnny's cat was an outside cat, and I could only imagine where she spent her time. I told my dad I was calling the doctor, and he planted himself on Johnny's couch while I worked through my phobia. The doctor said scratches needed only to be watched for infection. He asked when I had last received a tetanus shot, and, because it had been quite a while, the day ended with my getting a shot that left my arm sore. My husband wanted to know if the doctor thought I was crazy when he couldn't even find the mark on my hand. Feeling the need to tell my neighborhood girlfriends what had happened at our girls night out, the pain and embarrassment dragged on for days.

I was reminded of a short story by Ernest Hemingway entitled "Cat in the Rain." An American couple traveling outside of their homeland decided to make a stop at a particular hotel along the sea. The young wife noticed a cat hiding from the rain in the hotel's courtyard. She was determined to offer this cat a home with her. As the young wife dreamed about all the things she wanted in life, she decided that if she couldn't have them now, at least she could have this cat. More importantly, she felt terrible for the cat who was trying to take cover from the rain. She couldn't catch the cat, but by the end of the story, the hotel-keeper had the maid deliver the tortoiseshell cat to her. She remembered liking the way the hotel-keeper made her feel worthy of respect. She took notice of his aged appearance, a result from a hard working life, as seen in the shadows of his face and remembered his large hands.

I was sure that if I tried hard enough, I could find someone or something that would help me catch Hemme. I remembered husking corn with my Uncle Johnny on the back porch at a family birthday party. I remembered his hands and how they looked like my dad's. I prayed for a moment that his hands would pass Hemme over to me. Having a living piece of the farm would comfort me as I waited for my dream to become reality. Hemme brought me so many wonderful memories of my uncle, the farm, and his animals. She was the last one left.

When I left Hemme at the farm that day, she walked down the sidewalk to the front of the house, and I told her good-bye. This was the first time I had ever said good-bye to her. I always said I would see her later. At that moment, it rained redbirds. Two flew down off the gutter and another sat off in the distance. I understand now how important it is for us to follow God's will instead of our own. He understands our journey because He designed it. He knew when the time would be right to bring Hemme home, and He also knew that I had more work to do before that could happen. I realized I was telling her good-bye for now.

Nine months later, I found myself sitting at that same spot in prayer. Ralph was busy with work, and Hemme needed to be fed, so my weekly visits had turned into daily visits. I prayed for a moment of clarity rather than for a sign. I prayed for the commotion from all the opinions about Hemme to stop long enough for me to decide for myself what was right. Sometimes the right thing to do isn't always the easiest thing to do, but I can tell you, it is the easiest thing to live with. Your heart will always whisper that it was worth it.

My heart undoubtedly told me to give Hemme a chance with me. I had worried about leaving her at the farm with a new owner. I also imagined that she might run home from Ralph's farm and get hit on the road if I agreed to let him take her. I knew she and I had a connection, and she would be one of the last ways I would be connected to my Uncle Johnny. As she stared intently into my eyes, I needed to know that I had done everything I could to care for her.

The day finally came in October when it was the right time to bring her home. I had lined up a wonderful foster mom who would help with Hemme's transition. The vet was also informed that Hemme would be arriving shortly. I was nervous that day but for different reasons than on the day of the first failed attempt. The first time, I was concerned about whether I was doing the right thing. This time I was merely apprehensive about getting her in the carrier. It was a miserable, cold, and rainy day. I prayed that God and my uncle would be there with me. My plan was simply to place a can of moist cat food in the carrier and shut the door after she entered. We had been feeding her in the carrier for weeks. I pictured myself tripping, fur flying, and her running. My parents confidently waited in the car while I completed my mission. The carrier sat on the back deck with a fresh can of food waiting for her arrival. She quickly went in the carrier to eat, and I slowly reached over to shut the door. As I stood up from my chair to finish the job and completely secure the door, I was shocked by what seemed like a magnetic force pulling the door shut. I didn't have time to think about the divine intervention that had just occurred. In shock, I jumped in the car with my parents, and we were off to the vet.

The three weeks that Hemme spent in foster care were made so she could become adjusted to indoor life without my cats around. I didn't realize how that time would impart such an important transition in both of our lives. One week into Hemme's foster care, our family bulldog, Winka, passed away. Winka was the first pet Todd and I had as a married couple. After an incident with my son, however, we knew she was too nervous to be around small children, so she went to live with my parents. We became joint owners with my parents and consistently saw and cared for Winka over the years. Our whole family was heartbroken by her passing. I grieved for this loss as I would have grieved for a person. Once again, Sunny stayed by my side. I prayed that my uncle would take care of Winka while I took care of Hemme.

I began to understand where my connection with animals was coming from. Animals are God's creations, and each one is a piece of His heart. That is why we feel the unconditional love, guidance, and comfort they bring us. We are stewards who need to care for God's heart and His creations. We know what happens if we don't. I believe that in heaven, all His creations are brought back together the way they were meant to be. Isaiah 11:6 tells us:

"And the wolf will dwell with the lamb, and the leopard will lie down with the young goat, and the calf and the young lion and the fatling together; and a little boy will lead them."

That is why I know I will see my animal friends again. As I struggled with Winka's death, Allison told me I needed to trust in this belief. She reminded me to think back to that night in January when I believed Sunny showed me that animals can see God's face too.

Cats seem to come into our lives with a purpose. Most of the time, they seem to find us rather than our finding them. I know God is behind this plan. Hemme helped me say good-bye to the farm. She helped me feel safe as I sat alone in the middle of the ninety-acre property. Knowing that I wanted to live there someday, I needed to feel that assurance. She also helped me to accept the death of my beloved dog, Winka, and she will always help me keep a connection to my uncle. With everything she has given me, I am honored that I could give her a home that she loves, a new family, and two new feline friends. I discovered my "Ruby Tuesday;" it was the beautiful fall Tuesday in October when I finally brought Hemme home.

Living in the Moment

Our lives were different after Johnny passed away. I may have been the impetus; my transformation led our family to make changes. We volunteered together once a week, and I continued taking the kids to Johnny's to check on his place and enjoy the time we had left there. I'm grateful that my kids will always have those memories, but, little by little, the time had come to let go of his place because we had our own lives to live at our home in the suburbs.

It was spring and the kids played T-ball, softball, and basketball. Owen was going to play tackle football for the first time, and I cried at the thought of my baby getting pushed around, even though my mom thought he would be the one doing the pushing. He is the most sensitive little tough guy I know. In addition to sports, we were working to finish up the school year. Owen went to nature club where they explored many different animals and environmental issues. In one of the last weeks of class, a breeder brought in an Afghan dog. I looked forward to seeing the dog because when I was a child, Johnny had owned an Afghan dog. In all the years of nature club, there had never been an Afghan dog at the class. This was just another reminder of God's grace. Tears come in funny, unlikely places. I thought I would enjoy seeing the breed again. It had been about thirty years since I had last seen one. As soon as the dog came out of the crate, my eyes filled with tears. I felt as if I were five years old again, looking at my uncle's dog. With a distinct long narrow nose and shaggy fur long enough to touch the ground, this dog could not be mistaken. My mom always said that in the '70s, Johnny looked just like his Afghan because they were both tall, thin, and had long, shaggy hair.

Grief reminds us of how much we loved, so the experience of seeing the dog was bittersweet. I quickly left the building and cried all the way home. Todd was sitting on the couch, still in his work clothes, when I got there. He looked exhausted. I asked him if he could grab the camera and go to the church to take a picture of the Afghan. I knew he didn't want to go, but he did. He walked into the building and said, "I need to take a picture of a dog on a blanket. I'm short on time and have to be somewhere. My wife sent me. That's all I know." The group leader was completely confused until another mom said, "We have an Afghan dog, not a dog on an afghan." When Todd told me what had happened, I went from crying to laughing. I love those moments of humor that break into our hearts so unexpectedly.

Getting back to reality, my life was filled with the requirements of yard work, housework, and the constant need to run somewhere. In the past, I had been so uptight during this time of year, but now I was really trying to go with the flow and take everything in stride. Aware that the weeks, months, and years would pass by quickly, I knew I would miss this chaos when the kids were gone.

One morning, Owen came downstairs and saw two dirty socks that had been left on our kitchen stool the night before. The old me would have stayed up past midnight to wake up to a clean house, but my priorities were different now. I got a huge smile from Owen as he said, "Today must be my lucky day. I found two socks, and they match too!" He always got dressed by himself, but I usually got his socks and shoes for him. I told him how lucky he was, and the dirty socks went on his feet. We were always running late for everything, and this particular morning was no exception. I tossed a banana at him; that would be his breakfast. He moaned and groaned about it the entire way to the bus stop. I knew I had a long day ahead of me and hated to start the morning off this way, but I kept my composure. I'm sure he was loud enough on his own for the whole neighborhood to hear. We finally made it to Deb's driveway where he caught the bus. Deb's kids were not at the bus stop that day, and I would find out in the next moment that it was a good thing. Owen settled himself down long enough to ask me, "What did you pack me for a snack?" I hadn't had time to go grocery shopping for days because we had been so busy. At thirty-four years of age, I found myself terrified to answer a simple question from my six-year-old son.

My voice shook as I said, "A banana?" I could hear a little voice in my head that said, *"Prepare for impact."*

The explosion started with Owen's screaming, "I hate bananas!" He was always so easygoing, except on the rare occasion when he reached his breaking point. This would be one of those occasions. He took his book bag in his little hands and raised it high above his head. He then proceeded to slam it over and over again onto the concrete driveway. His face turned red, and then purple, as two tears streamed down his face. He looked as if he were operating a jackhammer.

I could only yell, "Owen, you are going to ruin your snack, and your juice box will explode!" We were saved by the bus that came rolling down the hill. "Thank God," I thought. I kissed both my children good-bye and watched Owen's tiny face stare at me through the bus window. In spite of having been upset moments ago, he waved and blew kisses to me until the bus disappeared at the bottom of the street. I know I will never forget that moment as long as I live.

Through all the screaming and chaos, Allison and Owen were my babies. Watching them grow up was a gift from God, and I was determined to enjoy every minute of it.

Letting Go

All I wanted for Mother's Day was a day of being off a schedule. It was ironic because as soon as you bring your newborn baby home, you are never off a schedule. I wanted to sleep in, be pampered, and then spend the day in the country at Johnny's. I awoke that morning to the classic breakfast in bed. With one frozen egg in our fridge, Todd couldn't make his famous pancakes. The kids carried in a tray of way-too-many carbohydrates, and I ate every last one of them with a smile. Owen gave me a poem with his handprint on it, and it made me cry. He didn't understand my emotional outburst, so he began to cry too. He thought I didn't like his gift. I know that someday, when he has children, he will understand that the simple things are the best things in life.

Allison gave me the book *Finding Grace* by Donna VanLiere. I first discovered one of her books, *The Angels of Morgan Hill*, as I walked through the library after Johnny had passed away. The cover depicted a simple farmhouse on a hill, which is what drew me to pick it up. That book just fell into my lap like so many other things in my life, and I believe it was God's plan. Within both books, the author's words were just another comforting whisper of God's grace.

Todd gave me a beautiful lap desk that would hold my laptop as I wrote my thoughts down. My parents gave me a picture of a young girl gazing out a barn window at a long, winding country road.

The little girl had a red ribbon tied in her hair, just like Grandma Susan had worn when she went running through the field to Aunt Kate and Aunt Suz's house as a little girl. Even though God may speak quietly, you can still hear His whisper. I was blessed with a wonderful family and I couldn't wait to spend the day with them at the farm.

We were going to take several pine trees that grew alongside my parents' back porch and replant them at the farm. We planned on positioning them at the bottom of the field we were trying to keep so that we could watch them grow over the years until the time came to make that field our home.

Owen loves hard labor. Once, when he was only five, he helped a landscaping company spread mulch at our neighbor's house. He'd stared at the workers until they finally invited him over. We were all proudly amused by his work ethic. I knew he would be enthusiastic about the project I had planned.

The boys dug the trees out, and we headed to the farm. Todd and Owen got started with the trees while Allison and I checked on the house. As we were walking back down the long driveway, Tucker, the neighbor's dog, came running toward us. Country dogs have a way about them. They have the freedom to roam, and Tucker always loved to chase the tires on moving cars as they made their way down to Johnny's. Ralph would get out of his truck and pet the black lab. All the members of the breakfast club received the Tucker welcome as they entered the farm on Sunday mornings. But for a long time, we didn't know if Tucker was friendly or not. One day, he made his way to us and immediately flopped on his back for a belly rub. He was our buddy from then on out, and the kids always looked for him.

Tucker had two new buddies to play with at his owner's farm; Johnny's neighbor, Heidi, had adopted two new labs. The puppies came barreling down the driveway a short time later, which was just another present for me to enjoy. We walked over to the field to see how things were going and were met by two beautiful horses.

Johnny always let his neighbors, Cindy and Barb, ride through the farm on their horses. He would invite them to stop in for a sandwich or refreshment, and they appreciated his kindness. It was quite a sight to see these magnificent creatures slowly approach us while making their way through the breathtaking country fields. Barb put Owen and Allison on her horse, Black Jack, while we took a few pictures. When they were about to leave, Barb asked if I wanted to get up on Black Jack. I hadn't been on a horse in over fifteen years. My immediate response was, "No thanks." Allison, who often seems to know what is best for me, said, "Mom, you should do it." I hopped up on Black Jack and took in the amazing view. They took a picture of me, but I should have taken a picture of what I was seeing from this perspective. Johnny once said, "There are some things your eyes will see that you will never forget." And he was right. A perfect little oak tree stood alone in the middle of this amazing open field. I hoped that tree would be the beginning of a bigger dream yet to come.

Cindy invited us to take the kids to see the new baby donkeys at her house. After the trees were planted, we went by and took some pictures of the newborn donkeys. Before we headed home, we got a bite to eat at a local restaurant along the river. It was quite a day. As an animal lover, I enjoyed several of God's amazing creations in every direction I turned. I couldn't have asked for a better day with my family if someone were to wrap the experience up and deliver it to me. Maybe someone did. It sure felt that way.

That day, I had a chance to meet Johnny's neighbor, Heidi. Her great-grandparents originally owned the farmhouse that Johnny had bought, and Heidi's dad had spent a lot of time there. My dad could still envision the elderly woman who had been sitting in the farmhouse when Johnny took a final walk-through. He was excited to start a life there, but she was so sad to leave. The property meant as much to Heidi as it did to me, which was hard to imagine. She had a deep appreciation for the land and wanted to keep it as untouched as possible. It was her treasure just as it was mine—and just as it had been Johnny's. It was a place of great history for both of us. I haven't met too many people in my life who share my name, and to think there may be two Heidi's living on a piece of land that means so much to both of them is something quite extraordinary. Perhaps it was meant to be. Speaking with Heidi gave me a small glimpse into the future. I told her that selling the house was the right thing to do for our family, but it would be like losing Johnny all over again. No house I had ever been in represented its owner better than Johnny's farm. His house seemed to live and breathe him with the antiques, pictures, and treasures of his life. I told her I couldn't imagine not being able to come back to the fifteen acres we were trying to keep.

During another visit to the farm, Heidi took us for a very slow ride on her quad to show us the view and pick wildflowers. I hope Owen remembers this ride the same way that I recall dune buggy rides when I was his age.

Heidi knew what it was like to lose something sentimental. She was blessed with many wonderful memories at her grandmother's cottage, but there came a day when it was sold and she couldn't go back. There will be many places that we can't return to in life, whether it be high school, college, or the house in which we grew up. Many chapters in life will eventually close, but new chapters will open. Standing on the hill, in the spot Todd told me would be the perfect place to build a house, I knew in my heart that I would be back. Like a young bride who knows when she finds her perfect wedding dress, I knew that I had found my home on this earth. I envisioned a yellow farmhouse with a front door painted deep red. I had only recently come to realize that under the worn-out brown paint on the front door of my uncle's yellow farmhouse lay shades of red.

Home is so much more than just a physical structure; it holds your family and your heart. The farm brought me the peaceful feeling of being at home. On one of my routine walks, I thought long and hard about my uncle and the farm. For one clear moment, I believed without a doubt that my uncle knew what would become of the farm, and it made him happy. Just as this thought came to me, I glanced up toward the top of the cemetery where I was walking and noticed the silhouette of a redbird standing about a foot high near a tombstone. With tears in my eyes, I made my way up the hill, and, sure enough, a decorative metal screen of a redbird stood proudly next to an American flag. I felt that my uncle understood my thoughts and was happy to know that we would continue to enjoy times at the farm spent with family and friends as we celebrated the joys of living.

The perfect ending to our Mother's Day visit to the farm occurred when Todd called to me to look at two butterflies fluttering through the long grass in the field. That sight was especially poignant, because my mom had given me a card that had been sent to the family after the funeral. On it was a picture of two butterflies: one was leaving, and the other was staying behind. I think they represented Johnny and me.

Epilogue

I was walking in our neighborhood on a beautiful afternoon, thinking about throwing a celebration of Johnny's life on October fifteenth, his birthday. Then reality set in; I didn't know if my family would still own the farm by then. Without hesitation, I realized that it didn't really matter because we should celebrate his life every day. At that moment, I looked up at the sky and saw a redbird sitting on a telephone wire directly above my head.

No one knows but God Himself what the future holds. He holds our plan in His hands, and we can only react to it and live it. As the Bible says, "Trust in the LORD with all your heart and do not lean on your own understanding" (Proverbs 3:5).

I called Allison's old riding instructor, who owns a horse farm, to see if she had any boarding clients looking for acreage. I didn't realize at the time that she was a real estate agent. Maybe she will become part of God's plan to help find the missing piece to this puzzle. I wanted more than anything to take some of the worry off my dad. I wrote on our prayer list at Bible study that I hoped that Johnny's place would be purchased by someone who would love the farm as much as he did. This would help give our family the closure we needed.

In my heart, it felt right that I should have my own farmhouse where I could display some of Johnny's beautiful things rather than place my things in his farmhouse. I suppose Johnny's farmhouse would always be his to me.

I know my uncle is fulfilled completely because he is with God, and that it makes no difference to him who will end up living in his earthly house. I will not build on Johnny's land just to make him happy that his farm has stayed in the family, but I do think it would make him happy to know that I love the farm for reasons of my own. Even if he were still living there, the farm would hold a special significance to me.

As I had lain grief-stricken in bed in the days following Johnny's death, I could have sworn I heard my uncle's voice say, "If I were there, I would love it." I couldn't understand what those words meant at that sad time, but I can now. I believe he meant that if he were still on this earth, he would approve of my dream for the property. Ricky hadn't been able to understand why I would want to build a house out at Johnny's place, but while accompanying my dad on a visit to the attorney's office, he said he now understood and that Johnny would be pleased to know my dream for the farm if he were here. Ricky wanted me to have what my heart desired.

When I was a little girl, Ricky had driven me on a dune buggy through the very field I wanted to keep. The "Words from the Master" that Johnny had penned on 4/20/08 read, "65 degrees, damp. What your eyes see in a split second, if shocking, dramatic, appalling, or jubilant, your brain will recall for a lifetime." That dune buggy ride was one of those times. I remembered feeling the air whipping through my fingers as my hands waved out through the bars of the dune buggy. We laughed and hollered as I yanked at the wildflowers that I still see in the field today. I was fearless. It was one of those magnificent moments I will remember all my life.

My uncle didn't leave anything specific in his will for me, and I didn't expect him to. In all honesty, my initial idea of living on his farmland began as a notion of convenience. It would be exciting to build our own home, especially because Todd is an architect and it has always been a dream of his. The price of the land would probably be right, and, on the surface, I loved the country and its poetic style. What had always been buried deep in my heart didn't completely surface until Johnny died. Maybe God brought us together that night in January so there would be nothing left unsaid.

My dad once questioned why he hadn't experienced God's grace and peace like I had. His turn eventually came. His heart just needed to be open to it. Sometimes we wait for what seems like too long, but grace always has perfect timing. Grace began to visit my dad almost daily in the form of a redbird tapping at his kitchen window in a face-to-face encounter. Our red-feathered friend would typically stop by every morning between 7:30 and 8:00, which just happened to be the same time that my dad used to check in with his brother John each day. I couldn't fully believe it until I experienced it myself, but that's often how grace works. Just as Hebrews 4:16 tell us, "Therefore let us draw near with confidence to the throne of grace, so that we may receive mercy and find grace to help in time of need." For my family, grace arrives on the wings of a redbird.

As I scripted the last thought of my story two days after my thirty-fifth birthday, I heard the song of what I knew could only be a redbird. I wished all along I had a witness on my journey, and finally Owen was able to share in what I saw. I followed the sound as we made our way to the front door of our house. A redbird sat on the railing of my narrow front porch—no more than two feet in front of us. We froze in place as the redbird chirped while intently looking at us for what seemed to be a very long time. We stared at the bird with only a glass storm door separating us. My uncle was a redbird in every right, with his red suspenders, red cheeks, and the best hair in the family—a perfect little crest. God painted him red, too.

In loving memory of John J. Broman

October 15, 1943 – January 1, 2010

I finally discovered the reason I was drawn so strongly to the farm. It is a spiritual home for my heart, full of what is simple and pure. It is a place where snowflakes fall like kisses from heaven, the moon lights up the sky like a halo, and the sun shines over us like a warm embrace. It captures the innocence of my childhood, the freedom of flying kites, and the enjoyment of dune buggy rides. It is a gathering place for family, where our souls will always be tied together. It is a constant reminder of that unforgettable night when you went home to heaven and the miracle that took place in my heart. To me, the farm will always be the closest thing to heaven on earth. And, as much as I love it, I love you more. ~Heidi

Dad and me

My favorite farm dog Boo and me

Dad, me, and Johnny on the front porch of the farmhouse

Dad and me flying a kite in the field

Cousin Trevor and me ready for a dune buggy ride

Ricky cutting one out of ninety acres

Todd, Allison, me, Dad, and Mom at the Broman family reunion

One of Owen's first visits to the farm

Fifteen acres and the start of a dream

"The bird also has found a house. And the swallow a nest for herself, where she may lay her young, even Your altars, O LORD of host, my King and my God." (Psalm 84:3)

Acknowledgements

T hank you, God, for never doubting me, for helping me write this story, and for the magnitude of Your creation. Every redbird you blessed me with has been a hug for my soul, leading me home.

Thank you, Johnny, for always being there.

Thank you, Ricky, for teaching me how to be fearless. I will never forget our dune buggy ride. RIP 08/21/13

Thank you, Dad, for the start of a dream and your constant love and support.

Thank you, Mom, for completing the first proofread and encouraging me to share my story. I could have never kept up with my life without you.

Thank you, Todd, for helping me with this project despite the late nights and technical difficulties. The kids thank you too for all of the good dinners and homework duty.

Thank you, Grandma Susan and Grandpap Evan, for watching over me and for the wonderful life you have created.

Thank you, Deb, for being one step ahead of me on my journey. You've helped to show me the way.

Thank you, Rose, for finding the cover for my book at the Bible study which played such a huge role in my life. We both know God was behind this blessing.

Thank you, Jack Puglisi, for generously lending me your amazing piece, "Winters Tale," for my cover. The quality of your work is extraordinary, and I am forever grateful.

Thank you, Vito, for your guidance and support with my first book and reminding me the importance of enjoying this moment.

Thank you, Scotty. As the sun sets and darkness lies upon the fifteen acres we kept from my Uncle John's farm, I will sit by our campfire under only the light of the moon and will never forget your advice: "Be afraid of what you see—not of what you don't see."

Thank you, Taressa Wills, for your legal advice and commitment to this project. Your expertise and kind heart have made the hardest part of this process easy.

Thank you, Patty Culbertson, not only for guiding me in Bible study but also in my writing, making it shine. Your endless commitment toward helping others is something I have learned from, and it will always be a part of my life.

Thank you, Meg Stefanac at MS Editorial Services, for preparing my manuscript for submission, for your friendship and support along the way, and for always making me laugh.

Thank you, Rick Bates and CrossLink, for this amazing opportunity. As a first-time published author, I could not have found a better partnership. Sharing this story has opened my eyes to my many blessings and God's purpose and plan for me.

Thank you, Dave and JJ Heller, along with Christian radio. Your music changed my heart.

> "And we know that God causes all things to work together for good to those who love God, to those who are called according to His purpose." (Romans 8:28)